LITTLE ONE-INCH

and Other

Japanese Children's Favorite Stories

To Aubrey on his
7th Birthday
13 June 1991

From your Mother with
Love

Annette M. Daniel

LITTLE ONE-INCH

and Other
Japanese Children's Favorite Stories

edited by
Florence Sakade

illustrated by
Yoshisuke Kurosaki

CHARLES E. TUTTLE COMPANY
Rutland, Vermont   *Tokyo, Japan*

Published by the Charles E. Tuttle Company, Inc.
of Rutland, Vermont & Tokyo, Japan
with editorial offices at Suido 1-chome, 2–6, Bunkyo-ku, Tokyo

© 1958 by Charles E. Tuttle Company, Inc.
All rights reserved

International Standard Book No. 0–8048–0384–6

First edition, 1958
Thirtieth printing, 1990

PRINTED IN JAPAN

Stories in This Book

Publisher's Foreword

In the autumn of 1953 we published the first edition of *Japanese Children's Favorite Stories from "Silver Bells,"* one of Japan's leading children's magazines. Since then, although the magazine is no longer published, the book has been so popular that successive reprintings have worn the plates past further use, and still orders pour in for it. To meet this continuing demand we have now issued a revised edition of the book with entirely new illustrations and several new stories, in a single volume entitled *Japanese Children's Favorite Stories,* and also in two companion volumes entitled *Peach Boy* and *Little One-Inch.* We are confident these books will meet the same enthusiastic response as did the first edition, and should like to quote the following remarks from the Foreword to that edition:

Parents and teachers all over the world have become increasingly aware of the need to raise their children to be citizens of the world, to become thinking adults who, while proud of their own traditions and heritage, are free of the national prejudices, rivalries, and suspicions that have caused such havoc in the past. To this end they have wanted material that would give their children a sympathetic understanding of the life and culture of other lands. This book will fill some part of this need.

We have chosen those traditional stories that may in a very true sense be called " favorites." They have been loved by the children of Japan for hundreds of years, and have proven no less delightful to Western children, thus showing again that the stories that please the children of one land are likely to please children everywhere.

Each of these stories is to be found in Japan—and often in other countries too—in many forms and versions. We have tried to select the most interesting version in each case and, in our translations, to remain true to the spirit of the Japanese originals. At the same time we have inserted sufficient words of explanation into the text of the stories to make customs and situations that are peculiar to Japan intelligible to Western readers without the need for distracting notes.

Editorial responsibility for the book has been borne by Florence Sakade; both as a mother and as an editor and author of numerous children's publications she has had wide experience in the entertainment and education of children. The English versions are the work of Meredith Weatherby, well-known translator of Japanese literature.

The Spider Weaver

LONG ago there was a young farmer named Yosaku. One day he was working in the fields and saw a snake getting ready to eat a spider. Yosaku felt very sorry for the spider. So he ran at the snake with his hoe and drove the snake away, thus saving the spider's life. Then the spider disappeared into the grass, but first it seemed to pause a minute and bow in thanks toward Yosaku.

One morning not long after that, Yosaku was in his house when he heard a tiny voice outside calling: "Mr. Yosaku, Mr. Yosaku." He went to the door and saw a beautiful young girl standing in the yard.

"I heard that you are looking for someone to weave cloth for you," said the girl. "Won't you please let me live here and weave for you?"

Yosaku was very pleased because he did need a weaving girl. So he showed the girl the weaving room and she started to work at the loom. At the end of the day Yosaku went to see what she'd done and was very surprised to find that she'd woven eight long pieces of cloth, enough to make eight kimono. He'd never known anyone could weave so much in just a single day.

"How ever did you weave so much?" he asked the girl.

But instead of answering him, she said a very strange thing: "You mustn't ask me that. And you must never come into the weaving room while I am at work."

But Yosaku was very curious. So one day he slipped very quietly up to the weaving room and peeped in the window. What he saw really surprised him! Because it was not the girl who was seated at the loom, but a large spider, weaving very fast with its eight legs, and for thread it was using its own spider web, which came out of its mouth.

Yosaku looked very closely and saw that it was the same spider which he'd saved from the snake. Then Yosaku understood. The spider had been so thankful that it had wanted to do something to help Yosaku. So it had turned itself into a beautiful young girl and come to weave cloth for him. Just by eating the cotton in the weaving room it could spin it into thread

inside its own body, and then with its eight legs it could weave the thread into cloth very, very fast.

Yosaku was very grateful for the spider's help. He saw that the cotton was almost used up. So next morning he set out for the nearest village, on the other side of the mountains, to buy some more cotton. He bought a big bundle of cotton and started home, carrying it on his back.

Along the way a very terrible thing happened. Yosaku sat down to rest, and the same snake that he'd driven away from the spider came up and slipped inside the bundle of cotton. But Yosaku didn't know anything about this. So he carried the cotton home and gave it to the weaving girl.

She was very glad to get the cotton, because she'd now used up all the cotton that was left. So she took it and went to the weaving room.

As soon as the girl was inside the weaving room she turned back into a spider and began eating the cotton very, very fast, just as though it were something very delicious, so she could spin it into thread inside her body. The spider ate and ate and ate, and then suddenly, when it had eaten down to the bottom of the bundle—the snake jumped out of the cotton. It opened its mouth wide to swallow the spider. The spider was very frightened and jumped out of the window. The snake went wriggling very fast after it. And the spider had eaten so much cotton that it couldn't run very fast. So the snake gradually caught up with the spider. Again the snake opened its mouth wide to gulp the spider down. But just then a wonderful thing happened.

Old Man Sun, up in the sky, had been watching what was happening. He knew how kind the spider had been to Yosaku and he felt very sorry

for the poor little spider. So he reached down with a sunbeam and caught hold of the end of the web that was sticking out of the spider's mouth, and he lifted the spider high up into the sky, where the snake couldn't reach it at all.

The spider was very grateful to Old Man Sun for saving him from the snake. So he used all the cotton that was inside his body to weave beautiful fleecy clouds up in the sky. That's the reason, they say, why clouds are soft and white like cotton, and also that is the reason why both a spider and a cloud are called by the same name in Japan—*kumo*.

Little One-Inch

THERE was once a married couple who had no children. One day they went to a shrine and prayed, saying: "Oh, please give us a child. We want a child so very badly." On their way home they heard a tiny crying sound coming from a clump of grass. They looked in the grass, and there they found a tiny little baby boy, wrapped in a bright red blanket. "This is the child that has come in answer to our prayers," they said. So they took the little baby home with them and raised him as their own son.

Now this baby was so tiny that he wasn't as large as a person's thumb, and even as he grew older he stayed the same size. He was just about an inch tall, so they named him Little One-Inch.

One day, when he had grown older, Little One-Inch said to his parents: "I thank you very much for raising me so carefully. But now I must go out into the world and make my fortune."

They tried to keep him from going, saying he was too tiny to go out into the world. But he insisted, so finally his parents said: "All right, we'll get you ready for the journey." So they gave him a needle to use as a sword, a wooden bowl to use as a boat, and a chopstick to use as an oar.

Little One-Inch got in his boat and waved goodbye to his parents, promising to come back when he'd made his fortune. Then he went floating down the river in his rice-bowl boat, paddling with his chopstick.

He floated for many, many miles, and then suddenly his boat was turned over. It was a frog in the river that had hit the boat. Little One-Inch was a very good swimmer. He swam to the bank and found himself standing before a great lord's house.

Little One-Inch looked at the house and saw that it must belong to a very wealthy lord. So he walked boldly up to the front door and called out. A manservant came to the door, but he couldn't see anyone.

"Here I am, down here," cried Little One-Inch. "Look down here."

The servant looked down at the floor by the front door. At first all he saw was the pair of wooden sandals that the lord used when he went out walking. Then the servant looked closer and saw the tiny figure of Little One-Inch standing beside the sandals. He was so surprised that he hurried off to tell the lord.

The lord came to the front door himself and looked at Little One-Inch, who was standing there very proudly, with his needle-sword at his hip.

"Why, hello there, little knight," said the lord. "What do you want here?"

"I've come out into the world to seek my fortune," said Little One-Inch. "And if you'll have me, I pray that you let me become one of your guards. I may be small, but I can fight very well with this fine sword I have."

The lord was very amused to hear a tiny boy use such bold words. "All right, all right," he said, "you can come and be a playmate for my daughter, the princess."

So after that Little One-Inch became the constant companion of the princess. They became very good friends, reading books and playing together every day. The princess made a bed for Little One-Inch in one of her jewel boxes.

One day the princess and Little One-Inch went to visit a temple near the lord's house. Suddenly a terrible green devil appeared, carrying a magic hammer. When the devil saw the princess he started trying to catch her. Little One-Inch drew his sword and began sticking the devil's toes with it. But the devil's skin was so thick that the tiny needle-sword wouldn't even go through it. The devil was getting nearer and nearer to the princess. So Little One-Inch climbed up the devil's body and out onto his arm. Then he waved the sword at the devil's nose. This made the devil so angry that he opened his mouth wide to give a big roar.

At that moment Little One-Inch gave a big leap and jumped right into the devil's mouth. Then he began cutting the devil's tongue with his sword. Now the devil's tongue was very tender and the needle hurt very much. He was so surprised at this that he spit Little One-Inch out onto the ground and went running away. He even dropped his magic hammer.

The princess ran and picked up the magic hammer. "Now we can make a wish," she said. Then she shook the hammer in the air and said: "Please let Little One-Inch grow taller."

And, sure enough, each time the princess shook the hammer Little One-Inch grew one inch taller. She kept right on shaking it until Little One-Inch was just as tall as she was. They were both very happy about this, and the lord was happy too when he heard what had happened.

When they were a few years older Little One-Inch and the princess were married and they lived very happily ever after.

The Badger and the Magic Fan

IN JAPAN goblins are called *tengu* and they all have very long noses. Now once upon a time three tengu children were playing in the forest. They had a magic fan. When they fanned their noses with one side of the fan, their noses would grow longer and longer, and when they fanned with the other side, their noses would shrink back to the original size. They were having a wonderful time fanning their noses back and forth.

23

Just then a badger came by and saw what they were doing. "My! how I'd like to have a fan like that!" he said to himself. And then he thought of a good trick. Because, you see, badgers are always playing tricks and can change themselves into any shape they want. So the badger changed himself into the shape of a little girl. He took a plate of bean-jam buns and went to the tengu children.

"Hello, little tengu children," said the badger. "I've brought you some wonderful bean-jam buns. Please let me play with you."

The tengu children were delighted, because they loved to eat bean-jam buns. But there were four buns to be divided among the three of them. And they immediately started arguing over who was to get the extra bun.

Finally the badger said: "I tell you what let's do. You all close your eyes, and the one who can keep his eyes closed and hold his breath the longest will win the extra bun."

They all agreed to this. The badger counted "One! Two! Three!" and the tengu children closed their eyes hard. As soon as they did this the badger grabbed up the magic fan and went running away with it as fast as he could, leaving the tengu children still holding their breath and keeping their eyes closed.

"Ha, ha, ha," laughed the badger. "I certainly made fools out of those tengu children."

The badger went on walking toward the city. Presently he came to a temple. At the temple he saw a beautiful girl dressed in very expensive clothes. He felt sure she was the daughter of a wealthy man, and in fact her father was the richest man in the country. So the badger crept up behind her on tiptoe. Quick as a flash he fanned her nose with the magic fan. Instantly her nose grew a yard long!

What a terrible to-do there was! Here was the beautiful little rich girl with a nose a yard long! Her father called all the doctors in the country,

25

but none of them could do anything to make her nose short. Her father spent much money on medicines, but nothing did any good. Finally in desperation the father said: "I'll give my daughter as a wife and half my fortune to anyone who can make her nose grow short again."

When the badger heard this, he said: "That's what I've been waiting for." He quickly went to the girl's house and announced he'd come to fix her nose. So the father took the badger to the girl's room. The badger took out the magic fan and fanned her nose with the other side of it. In the twinkling of an eye her nose was short again!

Her father was very happy and started making preparations for the wedding. The badger was very happy too because he was not only going to get a beautiful wife, but also a large fortune. On the day of the wedding there was a great feast. The badger was so happy that he ate and drank much too much and became very hot and sleepy.

Without thinking what he was doing, he lay back on some pillows, closed his eyes, and began fanning himself with the magic fan. Immediately his nose began to grow longer and longer. But he was half asleep and didn't see what was happening. So he kept on fanning and fanning and his nose kept on growing and growing. It went right up through the ceiling and on high up into the sky until it pierced the clouds.

Now, up above the clouds there were some heavenly workers building a bridge across the Milky Way. "Look at that!" they yelled, pointing to the badger's nose. "There's a pole just the right size for our bridge. Come, let's pull it up."

So they all began pulling on the badger's nose. How this surprised the badger! He started up out of his sleep, crying: "Ouch! Ouch! Help! Help!" And he began to fan his nose with the other side of the fan as hard as he could.

But it was too late. The workers kept on pulling him up, yelling: "Heave ho! Heave ho!" They pulled him all the way up into the sky, and no one ever saw him again.

Mr. Lucky Straw

ONCE upon a time, long ago, there was a young man named Shobei who lived in a farm village in Japan.

One day on his way home from working in the fields he tripped on a stone and tumbled over and over on the ground. When he stopped tumbling he discovered that he had caught a piece of straw up in his hand.

"Well, well," he said, "a piece of straw is a worthless thing, but it seems I was meant to pick this one up, so I won't throw it away."

As he went walking along, holding the straw in his hand, a dragonfly came flying in circles around his head.

"What a pest!" he said, "I'll show this dragonfly not to bother me!" So he caught the dragonfly and tied the straw around its tail.

He went on walking, holding the dragonfly, and presently met a woman walking with her little boy.

When the little boy saw the dragonfly, he wanted it very badly. "Mother, please get me that dragonfly," he said. "Please, please, *please!*"

"Here, little boy, I'll give you the dragonfly," Shobei said, handing the boy the straw.

To express her appreciation, the boy's mother gave Shobei three of the oranges she was carrying.

Shobei thanked her and went on his way. Before long he met a peddler who was so thirsty that he was almost fainting. There was no water anywhere near. Shobei felt very sorry for the peddler and gave him all the oranges, so he could drink the juice.

The peddler was very grateful, and in exchange he gave Shobei three pieces of cloth.

Shobei went on his way, carrying the cloth, and met a princess riding in a fine carriage guarded by many attendants.

The princess looked out of the carriage at Shobei and said: "Oh, what pretty cloth you have there. Please let me have it."

Shobei gave the princess the cloth and, to thank him, she gave him a large sum of money.

Shobei took the money and bought many fields with it. He divided the fields up among the people of his village. Thus everyone had a piece of land of his own. They all worked very hard in their fields. The village became very prosperous and many new barns and storehouses were built. Everyone was amazed when they remembered that all this wealth came from the little straw which Shobei had happened to pick up.

Shobei became the most important man in the village. Everyone respected him greatly. And as long as he lived they all called him "Mr. Lucky Straw."

Why the Jellyfish Has No Bones

LONG ago all the sea creatures lived happiiy in the palace of the Dragon King, deep at the bottom of the sea—well, almost happily. The only enemies were the octopus, who was the palace doctor, and the jellyfish, who back then had bones like all the other sea creatures.

One day the daughter of the Dragon King became sick. The octopus came to see her and said she would die unless she had some medicine made from the liver of a monkey. "The jellyfish can swim very fast," the octopus

said to the king, "so why don't you send him to get a monkey's liver?" So the king called the jellyfish and sent him on the errand.

But finding a monkey's liver wasn't easy. Even finding a monkey was difficult. The jellyfish swam and swam and swam. Finally one day near a little island he found a monkey who had fallen in the sea.

"Help! Help!" called the monkey, who could not swim.

"I'll help you," said the jellyfish, "but you must promise to give me your liver to make medicine for the Dragon King's daughter." The monkey promised; so the jellyfish took him on his back and went swimming away very fast toward the palace.

The monkey had been willing to promise anything while he was drowning, but now that he was safe he began thinking about it. And the more he thought the less he liked the idea of giving up his liver, even for the Dragon King's daughter. No, he decided, he didn't like the idea one little bit.

Being a very clever monkey, he said: "Wait a minute! Wait a minute! I just remembered that I left my liver hanging in a pine tree on the island. Take me back there and I'll get it."

So they returned to the island and the monkey climbed a high pine tree. Then he called out to the jellyfish: "Thank you very much for saving me. I can't find my liver anywhere, so I'll just stay here, thank you."

The jellyfish realized he'd been tricked. But there was nothing he could do about it. He swam slowly back to the palace at the bottom of the sea and told what had happened. The king was very angry.

"Let me and the other fish beat this no-good fellow for you," said the octopus.

"All right, beat him hard," said the King.

So they beat him and beat him until all his bones were broken. He cried and cried, and the wicked octopus laughed and laughed.

Just then the princess came running in. "Look!" she cried, "I'm not sick at all. I just had a little stomach-ache."

The octopus had planned all this so he could get even with his enemy, the jellyfish. The Dragon King became so furious that he sent the octopus away from the palace forever and made the jellyfish his favorite. So this is why the octopus now lives alone, scorned and feared by all who live in the sea. And this is why, even though he still has no bones and can no longer swim fast, the jellyfish is never bothered by the other creatures of the sea.

The Old Man Who Made Trees Blossom

ONCE upon a time there was a very kind old man and his wife living in a certain village. Next door to them lived a very mean old man and his wife. The kind old couple had a little white dog named Shiro. They loved Shiro very much and always gave him good things to eat. But the mean old man hated dogs, and every time he saw Shiro he threw stones at him.

37

One day Shiro began barking very loudly out in the farmyard. The kind old man went out to see what was the matter. Shiro kept barking and barking and began digging in the ground. "Oh, you want me to help you dig?" asked the old man. So he brought a spade and began digging. Suddenly his spade hit something hard. He kept digging and found a large pot full of many pieces of gold money. Then he thanked Shiro very much for leading him to so much gold, and took the money to his house.

Now the mean old man had been peeping and had seen all this. He wanted some gold too. So the next day he asked the kind old man if he could borrow Shiro for a little while. "Why, of course you may borrow Shiro, if he'll be of any help to you," said the kind old man.

The mean old man took Shiro to his house and out into his field. "Now find me some gold too," he ordered the dog, "or I'll beat you." So Shiro began digging at a certain spot. Then the mean old man tied

Shiro up and began digging himself. But all he found in the hole was some terrible smelling garbage—no gold at all. This made him so angry that he hit Shiro over the head with his spade, and killed him.

The kind old man and woman were very sad about Shiro. They buried him in their field and planted a little pine tree over his grave. And every day they went to Shiro's grave and watered the pine tree very carefully. The tree began to grow very fast, and in only few years it became very big. The kind old woman said: "Remember how Shiro used to love to eat rice-cakes? Let's cut down that big pine tree and make a mortar. Then with the mortar we'll make some rice-cakes in memory of Shiro."

So the old man cut down the tree and made a mortar out of its trunk. Then they filled it full of steamed rice and began pounding the rice to make rice-cakes. But no sooner did the old man began pounding than all

the rice turned into gold! Now th kind old man and woman were richer than ever.

The mean old man had been peeping through the window and had seen the rice turn to gold. He still wanted some gold for himself very badly. So the next day he came and asked if he could borrow the mortar. "Why, of course you may borrow the mortar," said the kind old man.

The mean old man took the mortar home and filled it full of steamed rice. "Now watch," he said to his wife. "When I begin pounding this rice, it'll turn to gold." But when he began pounding, the rice turned to terrible smelling garbage, and there was no gold at all. This made him so angry that he got his ax and cut the mortar up into small pieces and burned it up in the stove.

When the kind old man went to get his mortar back, it was all burned to ashes. He was very sad, because the mortar had reminded him of Shiro. So he asked for some of the ashes and took them home with him.

It was the middle of winter and all the trees were bare. He thought he'd scatter some of the ashes around in his garden. When he did, all the cherry trees in the garden suddenly began to bloom right in the middle of winter. Everybody came to see this wonderful sight, and the prince who lived in a nearby castle heard about it.

Now this prince had a cherry tree in his garden that he loved very much. He could hardly wait for spring to come so he could see the beautiful blossoms on this cherry tree. But when spring came he discovered that the tree was dead and he felt very sad. So he sent for the kind old man and asked him to bring the tree back to life. The old man took some

of the ashes and climbed the tree. Then he threw the ashes up into the dead branches, and almost more quickly than you can think, the tree was covered with the most beautiful blossoms it had ever had.

The prince had come on horseback to watch and he was very pleased. He gave the kind old man a great deal of gold and many presents. And, best of all, he knighted the old man and gave him a new name, "Sir Old-Man-Who-Makes-Trees-Blossom."

Sir Old-Man-Who-Makes-Trees-Blossom and his wife were now very rich, and they lived very happily for many more years.

The Crab and the Monkey

ONCE a crab and a monkey went for a walk together. Along the way the monkey found a persimmon seed, and the crab found a rice-ball. The monkey wanted the crab's rice-ball, and being a very clever talker, he finally persuaded the crab to trade the rice-ball for the persimmon seed. The monkey quickly ate the rice-ball.

The crab couldn't eat the persimmon seed, but he took it home and planted it in his garden, where it began to grow. Because the crab tended it carefully every day, it grew and grew.

The tiny seed finally became a big tree, and then one autumn the crab saw that it was full of beautiful persimmons. The crab wanted very much to eat the persimmons, but no matter how hard he tried, he couldn't climb the tree. So he asked his friend the monkey to pick the persimmons for him. Now, the monkey loved persimmons even better than rice-balls, and once he was up the tree he began eating all the ripe persimmons, and the only ones he threw down to the crab were green and hard. One of them hit the crab on the head and hurt him badly.

The crab was naturally angry and asked three of his friends, a mortar and a hornet and a chestnut, to help him punish the monkey. So these three friends hid themselves around the crab's house one day, and the crab invited the monkey to come to tea.

The Crab and the Monkey **45**

When the monkey arrived he was given a seat by the fire. The chestnut was hiding in the ashes, roasting itself, and suddenly it burst out of the fireplace and burned the monkey on the neck. The monkey screamed with pain and jumped up. At that instant the hornet flew down and stung the monkey. Then the monkey started to run out of the house, but the mortar was sitting up above the door and fell down with a thud on the monkey, almost breaking his back.

The monkey finally saw there was no escape. So he bowed down low to the crab and his three friends and said: "I really did a bad thing when I ate all Mr. Crab's good persimmons and threw the green, hard ones at him. I promise never to do such a bad thing again. Please forgive me."

The crab accepted the monkey's apology, and they all became good friends again. The monkey had learned his lesson and never again tried to cheat anyone.

The Ogre and the Cock

THERE was a mountain so high and steep that it seemed to touch the sky. And on top of the mountain there lived an ogre. He was a terrible ogre with blue skin and a single horn growing out of the top of his head, and he was always doing wicked things.

One morning the farmers living near the mountain went out to work in their fields and found all their vegetables ruined. Somebody had pulled

47

them up and trampled on them until there was not a single good one left. Who could have done such a thing? They looked very carefully and, sure enough, it was that wicked ogre. They could see prints of his big feet all over their fields.

This made the farmers very angry. They were tired of this ogre's tricks. They looked at all their ruined vegetables and became still angrier. Then they looked up at the mountain and all yelled at the same time: "O you wicked ogre! Why don't you quit doing these wicked things?"

The ogre looked down at them from the top of the mountain and answered in a terrible voice: "You must give me a human being each day for my supper. Then I'll quit bothering you."

The farmers had never heard of such an impudent ogre. They shook their tools at the ogre and roared: "Who do you think you are, wanting to eat a human being each day!"

"I'm the ogre-est ogre in all the land," the ogre roared back. "That's who I am! There's absolutely nothing I can't do! Ha! ha! ha!" The ogre's

48

voice echoed loudly through the mountains and made all the trees sway and toss.

"All right then," yelled the farmers. "Let's see if you're so wonderful. To prove it, in a single night you must build a stone stairway of one hundred steps from our fields all the way to the top of your mountain. If you can do that, then you can do anything and we'll just have to do whatever you want."

"I'll do it!" the ogre yelled back. "If I haven't finished the stairway before the first cock crows in the morning, then I promise to go away and never bother you again."

As soon as it grew dark that night, the ogre crept into the farmyard and put a straw hood over the head of every single chicken so they couldn't see when the sun began to rise. Then he said: "Now I'll build that stairway." And he set to work very hard, building a stairway right up the mountain.

He worked so hard and so fast that he already had ninety-nine steps in place. Then the sun began to rise in the east. But he only smiled to himself, thinking that the cocks wouldn't crow at all and that he'd still have plenty of time to put the last stone in place.

But there was also a good fairy who lived on the mountain. The fairy had been watching and had seen what a mean trick the ogre was playing. So while the ogre was going down for the last stone, the fairy flew down and took a hood off the head of one of the cocks.

The cock saw the sun rising and crowed loudly: *"ko-ke-kok-ko!"* This woke up all the other cocks, who had thought it was still night because of the straw hoods over their heads, and they all began to crow.

The ogre was very surprised when he heard this. "I've lost!" he cried. "And there was just one more stone to go." But even ogres must keep their promises, so he stroked his horn very sadly and went away far into the mountains.

No one ever saw the ogre again and the farmers lived very happily beside the mountain. They finished the stairway up the mountain and often went up it on summer evenings to enjoy the view.

The Rabbit Who Crossed the Sea

ONCE there was a white rabbit who wanted to cross the sea. Across the waves he could see a beautiful island and he wanted very badly to go there. But he couldn't swim and there were no boats. Then he had an idea.

He called to a shark in the sea and said: "Oh, Mr. Shark, which one of us has the most friends, you or I?"

"I'm sure I have the most friends," said the shark.

"Well, let's count them to make sure," said the rabbit. "Why don't you have your friends line up in the sea between here and that island over there? Then I can count them."

So the sharks all lined up in the sea, and the rabbit went hopping from the back of one shark to the next, counting, "one, two, three, four . . . " Finally he reached the island.

Then he turned to the sharks and said: "Ha, ha! You dumb sharks. I certainly fooled you. I got you to make a bridge for me, without your even knowing it."

The sharks became very angry. One of them reached up with his long snout and snatched off a piece of the rabbit's fur.

"Oh, it hurts!" cried the rabbit and began weeping.

Just then the king of the island came by. He asked the rabbit what was the matter, and when he'd heard the rabbit's story, he said: "You musn't ever fool others and tell lies again. If you promise to be good, I'll tell you how you can get your fur back."

"Oh, I promise, I promise," said the rabbit.

So then the king gathered some bulrushes and made a nest with them. "Now you sleep here in this nest of bulrushes all night," said the king, "and your fur will grow back."

The rabbit did as he was told. Next morning he went to the king and said: "Thank you very, very much. My fur all grew back and I'm well again. Thank you, thank you, thank you."

Then the rabbit went hopping off along the seashore, dancing and singing. He never tried to fool anyone again.

The Rabbit Who Crossed the Sea **55**

The Grateful Statues

ONCE upon a time an old man and an old woman were living in a country village in Japan. They were very poor and spent every day weaving big hats out of straw. Whenever they finished a number of hats, the old man would take them to the nearest town to sell them.

One day the old man said to the old woman: "New Year's is the day after tomorrow. How I wish we had some rice-cakes to eat on New

56

Year's Day! Even one or two little cakes would be enough. Without some rice-cakes we can't even celebrate New Year's."

"Well, then," said the old woman, "after you've sold these hats, why don't you buy some rice-cakes and bring them back with you?"

So early the next morning the old man took the five new hats that they had made, and went to town to sell them. But after he got to town he was unable to sell a single hat. And to make things still worse, it began to snow very hard.

The old man was very sad as he began trudging wearily back toward his village. He was going along a lonesome mountain trail when he suddenly came upon a row of six stone statues of Jizo, the protector of children, all covered with snow.

"My, my! Now isn't this a pity," the old man said. "These are only stone statues of Jizo, but even so just think how cold they must be standing here in the snow."

"I know what I'll do!" the old man suddenly said to himself. "This will be just the thing."

So he unfastened the five new hats from his back and began tying them, one by one, on the heads of the Jizo statues.

When he came to the last statue he suddenly realized that all the hats were gone. "Oh, my!" he said, "I don't have enough hats." But then he remembered his own hat. So he took it off his head and tied it on the head of the last Jizo. Then he went on his way home.

When he reached his house the old woman was waiting for him by the fire. She took one look at him and cried: "You must be frozen half to death. Quick! come to the fire. What did you do with your hat?"

The old man shook the snow out of his hair and came to the fire. He told the old woman how he had given all the new hats, and even his own

hat, to the six stone Jizo. He told her he was sorry that he hadn't been able to bring any rice-cakes.

"My! that was a very kind thing you did for the Jizo," said the old woman. She was very proud of the old man, and went on: "It's better to do a kind thing like that than to have all the rice-cakes in the world. We'll get along without any rice-cakes for New Year's."

By this time it was late at night, so the old man and woman went to bed. And just before dawn, while they were still asleep, a very wonderful thing happened. Suddenly there was the sound of voices in the distance, singing:

"A kind old man walking in the snow
Gave all his hats to the stone Jizo.
So we bring him gifts with a yo-heave-ho!"

The voices came nearer and nearer, and then you could hear the sound of footsteps on the snow.

The sounds came right up to the house where the old man and woman were sleeping. And then all at once there was a great noise, as though something had been put down just in front of the house.

The old couple jumped out of bed and ran to the front door. When they opened it, what do you suppose they found? Well, right there at the door someone had spread a straw mat, and arranged very neatly on the mat was one of the biggest and most beautiful and freshest rice-cakes the old people had ever seen.

"Whoever could have brought us such a wonderful gift?" they said, and looked about wonderingly.

They saw some tracks in the snow leading away from their house. The snow was all tinted with the colors of dawn, and there in the distance, walking over the snow, were the six stone Jizo, still wearing the hats which the old man had given them.

The old man said: "It was the stone Jizo who brought this wonderful rice-cake to us."

The old woman said: "You did them a kind favor when you gave them your hats, so they brought this rice-cake to show their gratitude.

The old couple had a very wonderful New Year's Day celebration after all, because now they had this wonderful rice-cake to eat.